Breakfast

by Janice Boland
pictures by Joe Veno

 Richard C. Owen Publishers, Inc.
Katonah, New York

This is the hen.

This is the egg.

This is John. Good morning!

John breaks the egg.

John cooks the egg.

Breakfast is ready.

"This is delicious!" says John.